It's Fun to Learn

Piglet's Night Lights

It was twilight in the Hundred-Acre Wood when Winnie the Pooh knocked on his good friend Piglet's door. Pooh was carrying a backpack with an enormous pot of honey sticking out of the top.

"Ready for our camp-out, Piglet?" Pooh called.

Piglet opened the door and looked around nervously. "Are you really quite sure about this, Pooh?" he asked. "It's getting awfully dark out there, and it's so light and cozy in here. Maybe we could just camp out in my living room."

"That would be a camp-IN, Piglet, not a camp-OUT," Pooh said.

Pooh reminded Piglet that their friends were waiting for them at the campsite.

"Everyone will be there, Piglet," Pooh said. "It's going to be splendid."

Pooh offered to help Piglet get ready. Pooh stuffed haycorn muffins into the pockets of Piglet's backpack while Piglet neatly packed his favorite blanket and teddy bear.

"I have the feeling I'm forgetting something, Pooh," Piglet said.

"Well, let's see," Pooh said. "We have honey." Pooh patted the sticky honey pot in his pack. "And we have plenty of haycorn muffins." Just to be sure, Pooh tucked two more particularly plump ones next to Piglet's teddy bear. "What else could we possibly need?"

Pooh and Piglet started for the campsite. As they walked, it got darker and darker, and Piglet got more and more nervous.

"What's that?" Piglet asked suddenly, pointing to a scary-looking shape in the trees.

"Well—I'm not certain, Piglet," Pooh answered. He was beginning to get a little bit nervous himself.

"Maybe if we snuggle up next to each other, it will go away," Pooh said.

"Maybe we should close our eyes, too," Piglet suggested.

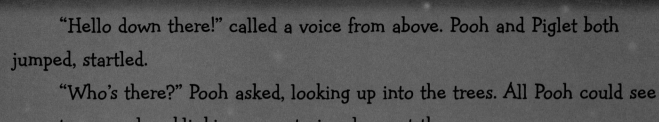

"Hello down there!" called a voice from above. Pooh and Piglet both jumped, startled.

"Who's there?" Pooh asked, looking up into the trees. All Pooh could see were two round, unblinking eyes staring down at them.

"Why, it's me—Owl," the voice answered.

"I thought you two might need a little help finding the others," Owl said. "We owls can see quite well at night, you know."

"Oh, thank you, Owl!" Piglet said.

"Lead on!" said Pooh, who was now feeling quite brave.

By the time the friends reached the campsite, it was completely dark. Pooh bumped into Rabbit, who was struggling to put up the tent.

"Well, don't just stand there," Rabbit said. "I need all the help I can get!"

"Did I hear someone say 'HELP'?" Tigger cried, bouncing into the clearing.
"Have no fear, Tigger's here! With illuminagination," he said proudly.

"Oh, and you brought a light, too!" cried Piglet, peeking out from under the
hood of his jacket. "Thank goodness."

With the lantern lighting the scene, the friends set up the tent. Piglet climbed inside and then poked his head back out.

"Oh, no!" Piglet cried. "I forgot my night-light!"

"I can't sleep without a night-light," Piglet said, wringing his hands. "What am I going to do?"

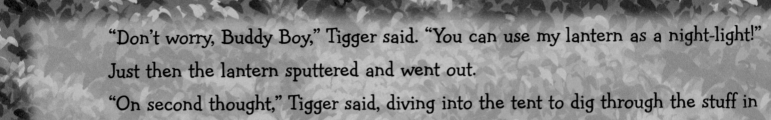

"Don't worry, Buddy Boy," Tigger said. "You can use my lantern as a night-light!"

Just then the lantern sputtered and went out.

"On second thought," Tigger said, diving into the tent to dig through the stuff in Rabbit's pack, "Long Ears must have something you can use."

In Rabbit's pack Tigger found a kite, a flowerpot and kitchen pans. He found garden tools and a bike horn. At the very bottom, he found a flashlight.

Tigger tried to turn it on, but nothing happened.

"This thinga-mabob's not working either!" Tigger cried.

At that moment, there was a crashing in the nearby bushes. It was Eeyore, carrying a load of branches on his back.

"Can't have a camp-out without a campfire," Eeyore said.

Everyone agreed wholeheartedly, and soon a cheerful fire was burning.

"Fire certainly is pleasant," Piglet said. "It makes a very good sort of light."

"It does a fantalicious job cooking marshy-mallows, too!" Tigger said, wrestling with a particularly gooey marshmallow.

"Fire is fine," Rabbit said. "But I think sunlight is the best light of all—because it makes my vegetables grow."

"I like the way the sun warms my tummy when I lie in the grass," Pooh said.

"And the colors when the sun sets are splendid," Piglet said.

"Look at that suspisherous-looking shadow on the tent!" Tigger shouted.

"That looks a lot like your tail to me," Rabbit said.

"Guess what this is?" Rabbit said, fluttering his hands like a butterfly.

"Why, it's a shadow puppet!" Owl said. "Isn't it remarkable what light can do?"

The friends played shadow puppets until bedtime. Then everyone went to bed—except Piglet, who wouldn't leave the light of the fire, and Pooh, who wouldn't leave his friend.

After a short while, the fire faded and went out. "Maybe we should go to sleep now, Piglet," Pooh said, yawning.

"I can't sleep without a night-light, Pooh," Piglet replied sadly.

Pooh thought very hard. "Think, think, think," he said, tapping his forehead to wake up any ideas that might be in there.

Just then a firefly landed right between Pooh's eyes. Crossing his eyes to see it, Pooh tumbled backward off the log he was sitting on.

Lying on his back looking up at the night sky, Pooh had an idea. "The stars are night-lights, Piglet," Pooh said, pointing up at the sparkling stars.

"And so are the fireflies," he added, smiling as a second one settled on his nose.

Piglet looked around him. "You're right, Pooh!" Piglet cried. "There are night-lights everywhere!"

Piglet pointed to the long path of moonlight shining on the surface of the lake. "Look at how bright the moon is tonight," Piglet said. "It's even brighter than my own night-light."

"Do you think you might be able to sleep now, Piglet?" asked Pooh with a huge yawn. "Piglet?"

But Piglet didn't answer.

He was fast asleep.

Fun to Learn Activity

I certainly saw different kinds of lights at our camp-out. There was everything from a lantern to fireflies!

Can you think of different kinds of lights inside and outside your house? What are they?